Honey's New Friend

For anyone who has ever
wanted a kitten – SM

STRIPES PUBLISHING
An imprint of Magi Publications
1 The Coda Centre, 189 Munster Road,
London SW6 6AW

A paperback original
First published in Great Britain in 2011

Text copyright © Sue Mongredien, 2011
Illustrations copyright © Artful Doodlers, 2011
Photographs copyright © iStockphoto.com, 2011

ISBN: 978-1-84715-153-7

A CIP catalogue record for this book is available
from the British Library.

Printed and bound in the UK.

10 9 8 7 6 5 4 3 2 1

Sue Mongredien

Kitten Club

Honey's New Friend

Stripes

Meet the Kitten Club girls!

Amy & Ginger

Mia & Smokey

Molly & Truffle

Ella
& Honey

Ruby
& Ziggy

Lily
& Buster

Chapter I

Ella Hughes was perched on the living room windowsill, eagerly gazing out at the street. It was Saturday afternoon, which meant only one thing: Kitten Club! Today's meeting was to be held at Ella's house, and her friends were due any minute. She smiled to herself, thinking about the surprise she and her mum had planned for the Kitten Club girls.

They were going to love it!

It was also the first day of the autumn half-term and Ella was excited at the thought of no school for over a week. She was really looking forward to some fun-packed days with her mischievous kitten, Honey. And Grandma was coming to stay too! It was going to be perfect.

Something tickled her bare feet suddenly, and she glanced down to see Honey jumping up at her toes.

"Hey," she said, hopping down to scoop her up. "Are you excited about Kitten Club too? Who do you think will get here first?"

Honey made a sound that was half-meow, half-purr as Ella stroked her. Then she spotted a fly buzzing around in the corner of the windowsill. She wriggled free of Ella's arms and scampered along to pounce on it. Ella smiled. Honey wasn't the sort of kitten who would sit still and be cuddled for ages – she wanted to play all day!

Then Honey caught sight of Misty, the family's other cat, curled up fast asleep on the sofa. The sofa was just about within leaping distance of the windowsill, and Honey crouched low, quivering with excitement, her eyes fixed on the dozing older cat.

Just in time, Ella realized what her lively kitten was planning. "Oh no you don't," she said, and grabbed hold of Honey quickly. "Jumping on Misty is *not* a good idea!" she added, stroking her kitten's soft little head.

Honey gazed up at Ella with her big green eyes, as if the thought had never crossed her mind. Ella giggled. Honey really was a troublemaker sometimes, and loved pouncing on Misty's tail or chasing after her.

Honey was just being playful – she was only a kitten, after all – but Misty would get very bad-tempered at being woken up or leaped on, and would sometimes lash out or growl at Honey. In fact, Ella thought, as Honey jumped out of her arms in pursuit of the buzzing fly again, it was a miracle that her kitten and cat were in the same room together, without there having been a fight yet.

Just then, Ella caught sight of Mia walking up the road with her dad, and waved excitedly through the window at her. Oh, and there was Molly's mum's car, dropping off Molly, Ruby and Lily too. Ella picked up Honey and rushed to open the front door. Kitten Club was about to begin – hurrah!

"Hi, everyone!" Ella said as her friends trooped into the house. "Oh, is that Amy's car pulling up as well? Brilliant, we're all here."

The six girls had met back in the summer, when they were choosing kittens from Chestnut Farm. They'd all really hit it off, so Lily had suggested forming a club together ... and Kitten Club had begun!

"Hi, Ella, hi, Honey," Mia said, hanging up her coat. "Brrr, it's cold out there today."

"It's just started to rain too," Amy said, taking off her boots and standing them neatly by the radiator. "Hi, everyone! Hello, Honey – what a wriggler you are!"

Ella laughed. "I think she's impatient to get Kitten Club started," she said. "Shall we go through to the living room? I've set everything up in there."

She led them through. Ella had spread some cushions on the floor, and brought down her beanbag from her bedroom so that everyone could gather round the Kitten Club scrapbook. Earlier, her dad had helped her make a tray of drinks for everyone, and they'd also put out some mini muffins and red grapes on a plate.

"Oh, we've got Misty *and* Honey in with us today," Lily said, walking over to where Misty was still fast asleep. She stroked her gently and Misty opened her eyes a crack, then shut them again.

"Hello, Misty," said Molly, going over to stroke her too. She smiled. "Doesn't she look big? You get so used to having a dinky little kitten that grown-up cats seem like giants all of a sudden."

"I kept thinking that when we first got Honey," Ella agreed, putting Honey down on the carpet. "Misty's paws suddenly seemed as big as shovels next to Honey's titchy ones." She grinned as her kitten wandered over to Ruby, who was sitting on

the floor nearby, and started batting interestedly at the beaded bracelet on her wrist. "Watch out, Rubes, kitten alert!"

Ruby giggled and stroked Honey. "Hey you, that's a bracelet, it's not a cat toy," she said.

The girls sat in a circle on the floor, and Ella passed round the muffins.

"Yum," said Amy, biting into a chocolate one. "Shall we get started then? Where's our scrapbook?"

Ruby produced it from her bag and opened it up on her lap. "It's getting quite full now," she said, flicking through the pages they'd already filled. Every week, the girls wrote in all their kitten news, and stuck in any photos or pictures. A lot had happened since their first meeting back in the summer!

Ruby found the next empty page and neatly wrote the date. "OK, time for our roll-call," she said with a grin. "Tomboy?"

"Meow!" said Ella, answering to her secret club name.

"Witch-Cat?"

"Meooooow!" yowled Mia, pulling a spooky face, which made everyone laugh.

"Moggy?"

"Meow-oh!" said Molly, jumping as

Honey attacked the hem of her trousers.

"Scatty?"

"MEOW!" replied Lily dramatically, holding up her hands like paws. Both Misty and Honey turned to stare at her in surprise for a moment, and everyone burst into giggles. Lily was *so* going to be on stage when she was grown up, Ella thought to herself with a grin. Misty blinked, and then settled back down to sleep.

"Green-Eyes," Ruby said.

"Meow," Amy replied.

"And Glamour-Puss – that's me," Ruby said, ticking herself off. "Let's get this meeting started! What's everyone's news this week?"

"Well," Molly began, but before she could say anything else, Finn, Ella's twin brother, burst into the room with his friend Lucas.

"I'm *so* going to beat you," Finn said to Lucas as he switched on the TV and PlayStation, ignoring the girls. "I've been practising loads for this. Bring it on!"

Ella bristled. Finn was such a pain! Couldn't he see that they were using the living room? "Hey, we're having a meeting," she said. "Go and play somewhere else."

The TV blared thunderous music as the boys' game began loading. Finn ignored Ella and tossed one of the game controllers to Lucas, taking the other for himself. Then they both sat on the sofa, making Misty's ears prick up in annoyance.

"Finn!" Ella said. "I'm talking to you!"

"Yeah, yeah," he said. "Whatever."

"Welcome to … JUNGLE WARS!" boomed a deep voice from the TV. "Prepare for battle."

Finn sniggered as Honey bounded across the room and leaped on to his feet. "Welcome to … CAT WARS!" he said, picking up Honey and whizzing her through the air.

"Finn, *don't!*" Ella cried, jumping up in alarm.

"Prepare for battle," Finn said, and plopped Honey right on to Misty's back.

Misty yowled and lashed out crossly at Honey, who almost fell off the sofa in her hurry to run away. Both boys burst into guffaws of laughter.

Ella picked up Honey and cradled her, feeling furious with her brother. "You could have hurt Honey, doing that. And now you've upset Misty too, when I'm already having trouble trying to help Misty and Honey be friends. Good one," she snapped sarcastically. She turned to her friends, still prickly with rage. "Come on, girls, let's go upstairs, away from these idiots."

"Whatever!" called Finn in an irritating sing-song voice as they left the room.

Ella stalked upstairs, clutching Honey to her chest. "BOYS!" she muttered.

Chapter 2

Up in her bedroom, Ella took a while to calm down. "My brother is so annoying!" she fumed, her fingers trembling as she stroked Honey. "Why does he have to stir up trouble like that? It drives me mad!"

"Boys are pains," said Molly, who had three brothers of her own. She put an arm round Ella, and they both petted Honey for

a minute. Mia passed Ella her drink that
she'd brought up for her, and Ruby, who'd
remembered to bring the plate of muffins,
handed them round.

"Thanks, guys," Ella said, her anger
draining away. "Let's try again. What's
everybody's news?"

The club members swapped stories
about their kittens, and wrote them into the
scrapbook. "How about you, Tomboy?"
Amy said after a while. "What have you and
Honey been up to this week?"

"Well, most of the time I've been trying
to stop this little minx fighting with Misty,"
she replied, tickling Honey under the chin.
"Poor Honey just wants to play, but Misty
likes sleeping for hours and hours and
Honey gets on her nerves. It's really tricky."

Lily looked thoughtful. "You know …
when Jessica was born, I wasn't all that keen
on her at first," she said. "It seemed like
Mum and Dad gave her all the attention,
and I felt as if they didn't love me as much
as her." She shrugged. "I know now that
really they love us both the same, but what

I'm trying to say is that maybe Misty needs some extra TLC, so that she knows *she's* still loved."

"That's a good idea," Ella said. "Maybe we *have* given Misty less attention since Honey's come to live with us. I'll be extra-nice to her this week."

"You could try putting a bell on Honey's collar too," Ruby suggested. "We've got one on Ziggy's collar so that the birds will hear him out in the garden and know to fly away. And if Honey's jingling around the place, it'll give Misty some warning that there's a kitten nearby."

"That's another good idea," Ella said, feeling more cheerful. "Thanks, guys. I'll try both those things. Hopefully they'll help with the problem."

There was a knock at the door just then, and Ella's mum popped her head into the room. "Hello everyone," she said. "Sorry not to see you earlier, but I've only just got back from work. Ella, I'm ready to do the You-Know-Whats when you are."

Ella smiled. She'd almost forgotten about the surprise she and her mum had planned for the others, she'd been so mad with her brother. "Oh yes," she said. "Thanks, Mum. We'll do it now. Come on, everyone. Downstairs again!"

"What's happening? Where are we going?" Mia asked, jumping off Ella's bed at once.

"Aha," Ella said mysteriously as she led them back downstairs. "Wait and see."

Ella and her mum took the girls into the kitchen, where the table had been covered with newspaper, and lots of different pots of paint had been set out. Ella's friends gave an "Ooooh!" of excitement, and her mum smiled.

"I don't know if Ella's told you, but I run the pottery-painting café in town," she said. "And we thought it might be a nice idea if we had our own Kitten Club pottery-painting session here at home. I've brought you all a door plaque to decorate and we've got lots of different paint colours. I'll fire the plaques for you during the week, and Ella will bring them to your next meeting. How does that sound?"

"That sounds totally cool!" Mia said happily. She loved drawing and painting. "Thank you so much!"

"Great," Amy said, her eyes shining. "What a fab idea!"

The girls sat round the table and began to paint. Ruby chose a pink background for her door plaque, then painted "Kitten Lover" on it in silver swirly letters. Molly painted football stripes on hers, with "Molly's Bedroom" and a row of kitten-sized paw prints along the bottom. Ella painted her plaque blue, with "No Boys Allowed" in big letters.

They chatted as they painted, while Honey chased a ping-pong ball around their feet like a mad thing, making the girls giggle whenever she brushed past them. "So what are you all up to over half-term," Lily asked, dipping her paintbrush into the gold paint. "We're off to stay with my grandma and grandpa for a few days tomorrow," she continued. "Our neighbours are looking after Buster while we're gone – they've promised to give him lots of cuddles, but I'm going to miss him so much." She pulled an anguished face and Ella smiled to herself. Lily was always such a drama queen!

"My cousins are coming to stay," Mia said, carefully adding a purple swirl to her plaque. "They're really fun – and Mum said they're dying to meet Smokey."

"And it's Halloween at the end of the week too, isn't it?" Molly said. "I can't wait. I love Halloween." An excited look came over her face. "Hey! We should have a Halloween party at our next Kitten Club meeting, shouldn't we? I'm sure my mum will say it's OK to have it at our house."

"Ooh yes," Ella said at once. "We could all make special costumes and dress up. Brilliant!"

"I bet Grandma will help you with a costume," Ella's mum said, overhearing their conversation. "She's really good at making things."

Ella smiled. "That's a great idea."

"And we can play Halloween games at the party," Amy put in enthusiastically. "Ooh, and tell spooky ghost stories too!"

As the girls discussed a Halloween Kitten Club and all the fun things they could do together, Misty slunk into the kitchen, looking as if she'd had quite enough of the boys' noise. Honey made an excited leap towards her, startling the older cat. Misty hissed, her tail fluffing up like a bottle brush, then scuttled out through the cat flap. It was still raining outside and she sheltered under a bush, looking thoroughly miserable.

"Poor old Misty," Ella said, watching her. It was awful that Misty preferred sitting out in the rain to being in the house with Honey. She made a vow there and then that her half-term project was to make Misty feel happier, and to persuade the two cats to be friends. She would brush Misty's long grey fur every day and find something extra-yummy for the old cat to have for tea. Project Happy Cats would start right away!

Chapter 3

That evening, over dinner, Ella told her
family her plans for keeping the peace
between the two cats, and hopefully
building a friendship. Her mum nodded.
"That all sounds very sensible," she said.
"Now that it's half-term, you should have
more time to play with Honey, which means
she won't be bothering Misty all the time."

"I'll go to the pet shop tomorrow and pick up a collar with a bell on it," Dad added. "It will give us all a bit of warning that Honey's in the area... She pounced on my foot earlier, and I nearly fell over in shock!"

Finn had been quiet throughout this conversation and Ella pointed her fork at him. "And no more cat wars, thank you very much," she said shortly. "That just makes everything ten times worse."

"Yeah, yeah, whatever," Finn said, pulling a face. "Honestly – girls!"

SUNDAY

Started Project Happy Cats today!
Dad got Honey a new collar with a bell
on and she now jingles and jangles
wherever she goes - every time she
hears it, Misty's ears prick up and off
she runs. Still, it's better than them scrapping all the
time, I suppose!

I spent ages playing with Honey today - it was such
fun. I made some tunnels for her out of old newspaper
and she loved going through them ... and
then attacking the newspaper and ripping
it to shreds! She had her mad face on -
it really made me laugh. Then she

Mad!

was worn out and fell asleep on my bed,
so I went and gave Misty a lovely long
grooming session, brushing her coat for
ages. She purred and purred.

Grandma's going to be here in the
morning - I can't wait to introduce her to Honey!

Ding-dong!

"Could you get that, Ella?" her mum called. "I'm on the phone."

"Sure," Ella said, scrambling off the sofa where she'd been playing with Honey. She ran to the front door, opened it and beamed. "Grandma!" she said happily, throwing her arms round her.

Grandma gave Ella a big squeeze. She smelled of lavender and peppermints, and always gave the best hugs. "Hello, sweetheart," she said. "Lovely to see you. I've thought of all sorts of fun things we can do together while I'm here … and I've brought my bag of tricks too!"

Ella smiled. Grandma was one of those people who was constantly busy, and who never sat still. She couldn't even watch the

TV without knitting or sewing or doing a tapestry. Her "bag of tricks" was always full of arts and crafts things, and there was usually some cool stuff in there, like unusually-shaped buttons, masses of bright embroidery thread, or pieces of beautiful fabric. "Sounds good to me," Ella said happily. "Do you think there might be something in your bag of tricks that I could use for a Halloween costume?"

Grandma's eyes twinkled. "I'm sure we can find something spooky in there," she said. "Now, where's this kitten of yours?

I've been dying to meet her!"

Ella took Grandma through to the living room, but just as they walked in, both Honey and Misty shot out. Misty looked thoroughly fed up as she tried to escape from Honey, who was chasing after her, frantically trying to pounce on Misty's tail.

"Oh, Honey!" sighed Ella, running after her kitten and making a grab for her. Misty shot outside, where it had just started drizzling. Ella gave Grandma a sad smile. "As you can see, Honey and Misty aren't getting on brilliantly, but I'm working on it."

Ella's mum came in then, and Finn sloped in to say hello, and soon after that it was time for lunch. Poor Misty stayed out in the rain the whole time, and Ella felt terrible. She had to try harder with Project Happy Cats!

WEDNESDAY

It has been raining non-stop since Monday -
arrgh! Grandma took us to the cinema
yesterday, and we went swimming this morning, but
the rest of the time we've been cooped up indoors.
Finn is driving me nuts, moaning
about how bored he is.

Grandma had some black
crêpe paper in her bag so we
made a cardboard witch's hat
then covered it with the crêpe
paper. I've stuck silver moons
and stars on it too, and it looks really cool.
She said we can pick up some black sparkly fabric
for a dress and cape next time we go into town.
If the rain ever stops!

This afternoon, we made cookies with Grandma
but Finn got in a strop and threw a
handful of flour at me when I told him
to stop stealing the chocolate chips.

Then Grandma told him off, and he went off in a sulk, and THEN we heard him shout "Cat wars!" and start a fight again with Honey and Misty. I could've killed him!

Even worse, when I tried to break up the fight, I got scratched by Misty. OW. It still really hurts. It's all my stupid brother's fault!

One good thing is that Misty really likes Grandma. She cuddles up on her lap every evening, purring and purring, while I keep Honey distracted by playing with her. So Grandma is helping with Project Happy Cats, even if Finn isn't!

On Thursday, the rain stopped, so Grandma took Ella and Finn to the adventure playground, where they bumped into some friends from school. Then on Friday they finally went shopping, and Grandma took Ella into a shop that sold lots of different fabrics. Ella found one which was black with tiny golden stars scattered throughout. She held up the roll, beaming. "Look! This will be perfect for my witch's costume!" she said.

"A witch sounds about right," Finn muttered, earning himself a kick from Ella. "Ow! Grandma, she kicked me!"

Grandma rolled her eyes and laughed. "As well as a witch dress, we need some witch *magic* to stop you two arguing," she said. "Honestly!"

Once they got home, Grandma measured Ella, and drew out a pattern on the black material. Ella helped cut the material to the right shape and chose a large midnight-black button from Grandma's bag that would be perfect for holding the cape together.

"You're going to be the best-dressed witch there has ever been," Grandma said with a wink, as she threaded her needle.

Ella hugged her. "You're the best *grandma* there has ever been," she said, feeling excited about her costume.

Later that day, Ella went round to Amy's house for tea. It felt good to get away from her brother for a bit. Amy was fairly new to the area, but both girls had horse-riding lessons together at the weekend, and Ella had enjoyed getting to know her. And her marmalade-coloured kitten, Ginger, was absolutely adorable too!

"Have you got your Halloween costume ready yet?" Amy asked as they went upstairs to her bedroom, with Ginger scampering along behind them.

"Nearly," Ella said. "Grandma's helping me make it. I'm going as a witch — how about you?"

"I'll show you," Amy said, as they entered the bedroom. "Close your eyes while I put it on so that I can surprise you. Ginger, you close your eyes too. No peeping!"

Ella obediently shut her eyes, but it didn't sound as if Ginger had from the way Amy kept giggling. "Hey you," she said. "Paws off!"

Then Ella heard a zip being pulled up. "OK," Amy said. "Ready!"

Ella opened her eyes to see Amy in a velvety black catsuit, with a long black tail attached at the back. Amy got down on all fours and grinned. "And for the finishing touch…" she said, slipping a cat mask over her face. "Meow!"

Ginger had been sniffing at the catsuit with interest, but as soon as Amy put on the mask and meowed, he shot backwards so fast that he almost did a somersault. His green eyes were wide with shock, and the next moment he bolted from the room.

Amy and Ella burst out laughing. "Oh dear!" Amy spluttered. "Poor Ginger! He looked as if he really thought I was a gigantic cat! I'd better take it off again."

"You look fab!" Ella said, still giggling. "And at least we know it's realistic. I'll go and find him – make sure he's OK. Ginger!" she called, walking out of the room.

Ginger was on the landing. He looked relieved to see Ella and pattered over to her,

pressing himself against her legs. "It's OK," Ella said, scooping him up and stroking him. "The big cat's gone now. Don't worry."

Despite Ella's reassuring words, Ginger stiffened in her arms as they went back into the bedroom. He looked around for the big cat, then jumped on to the floor and sniffed all around the bedroom very suspiciously.

Amy was now back in her ordinary clothes and stroked him lovingly. "Don't worry," she said. "You're the only cat for me."

Ella smiled as Ginger broke into a loud, rumbling purr and squeezed his eyes shut happily, enjoying being stroked. She couldn't help feeling that it must be nice for Ginger, being the only cat in the house. Misty would probably feel *very* jealous of him right now, if she could see him!

Chapter 4

"There!" said Grandma, putting the witch's hat on Ella's head. "What do you think?"

Ella looked at herself in her parents' full-length mirror and grinned. It was Saturday afternoon and she was all dressed up for the Kitten Club Halloween party. Grandma had made her a dress and cloak from the black, sparkly fabric, which Ella

was wearing with some purple and black stripey tights. Mum had borrowed a long black wig from one of her friends too, which completely covered Ella's blonde hair, and Ella had bought a large rubbery nose from the fancy-dress shop.

"I love it," Ella said, giggling at her reflection. "It doesn't look like me at all. I'm so … spooky!"

Her mum smiled. "Go on, give us a witch's cackle," she said.

Ella turned and pulled a face at them. "Ha ha ha ha HA!" she cackled witchily, and Mum and Grandma both laughed.

"Let me just add the finishing touches with this," her mum said, picking up a brown eyeliner pencil. She leaned close to Ella's face and drew some small brown

circles on her chin and by her nose. "There. Warts," she said. "Perfect."

"Look, here's Honey come to inspect your costume," Grandma said, as the inquisitive kitten padded into the room. "What do you think, Honey?"

Honey stopped dead when she saw Ella and gave a surprised-sounding meow, as if she didn't recognize her.

"It's me!" Ella laughed, bending down to stroke her. She pulled off her fake nose to show Honey. "Look, silly."

Grandma smiled. "It's a shame you can't take her along with you. Every witch needs her cat, doesn't she?"

"Amy will have to do instead," her mum said. "Now, where did I put those Kitten Club plaques? I'll just find them, then you'd better go."

Ella gave Honey a last stroke. "Be good while I'm out," she said. "Be nice to Misty!"

"I'll keep an eye on them," Grandma said. "Project Happy Cats is safe with me!"

Ella's dad dropped her and Mia – who was in a wizard costume, complete with fake

beard – off at Molly's. Their meeting was starting a bit later than usual, as Molly's mum had said they could all stay on for a party tea after they'd played some Halloween games. Ella felt jumpy with excitement as they got to Molly's house. It was always brilliant to see her Kitten Club friends – but it was even better when there was a party too!

Molly answered the door … and Ella and Mia both burst out laughing when they saw her. Molly was wearing a bright orange dress with green tights, and had a pumpkin face-mask, with triangle-shaped eyeholes and crooked cut-out teeth. "You're a pumpkin!" Ella cried. "What a cool costume!"

Molly grinned under her mask. "Yours are great too," she said. "Come in. The others are

in the kitchen with Truffle. She's having a lovely time playing with Amy's tail."

In Molly's kitchen there was a ghost (wearing shoes just like Ruby's) and a skeleton (with a laugh just like Lily's) tucking in to cheese and crackers, as well as two cats – one large and suspiciously girl-shaped, and one teeny tabby one.

"Hi everyone," Ella said. "Whoa, Lily, you are *bony*, girl! You need to eat more of that cheese!"

Lily – who, as a skeleton, had white bone shapes pinned all over her – laughed. "Don't worry, I'll fill up on the party food later. Or maybe I'll just snack on that big pumpkin behind you if I get really hungry!"

Ella laughed, then put the box of plaques carefully on the table. "I've got a surprise for you all," she said, lifting the lid. "Ta-dah!"

Everyone crowded round as she unpacked the plaques and handed them out. "Ooh! They look great," Mia said, then promptly sneezed three times. "Sorry," she said. "I think this beard must be dusty. Either that or I'm – *atchoo!* – getting a cold."

The girls' meeting began as usual with the roll-call and their Kitten Club news.

Truffle sat on Amy's lap, happily purring throughout, and Amy wound her long black tail around her, which made everyone laugh.

"Truffle, you're much braver than Ginger," Amy said. "He freaked out when he saw me in this costume, didn't he, Ella?"

"He was terrified," Ella agreed. "But Truffle doesn't seem bothered one bit. In fact, I think you're her new best friend, Amy."

"Smokey's made a new friend too," Mia put in. "There's a black and white cat next door, and Smokey thinks she's the best thing ever! Whenever she comes into our

garden, he gets all excited and starts showing off, running up trees and trying to climb the fence." She laughed. "I think he's a bit in love with her, actually."

"Ahhh," Ella said, smiling. "How sweet! There's a cat who lives near us too – Nero, he's called – this great big tom cat. He's a bit of a thug, I think, and Misty and Honey aren't very keen on him. That's one thing they agree on, at least."

Lily had brought a photo of her kitten Buster in the middle of a huge pile of brown and yellow leaves in their back

garden, looking extremely happy. "Buster's had a great time all week chasing the falling leaves.

He just loves them! Every time Mum or
Dad try to rake them up, he wants to
join in, pouncing on all the stray ones.
It's so cute."

"Ziggy likes them too," Ruby said, lifting
off the white sheet that was her ghost
costume, and draping it round her shoulders
so that she could see her friends better.
"Now that he's Mr Confident about going
outside, he charges about like a loon
whenever the wind is blowing the leaves
off the trees."

Ella pulled a face. "Honey's favourite
thing to attack is still Misty!" she sighed,
propping her chin up in her hand. "Leaves
aren't as much fun as Misty's tail."

Molly, who was sitting next to Ella,
peered closely at her hand. "Ouch," she

said, looking at the scratch. "And who did this?"

"Misty," Ella replied. "I was trying to stop them having a fight, and my hand got in the way. I just wish they could be friends!" She pulled a face. "It was my half-term project to try to help them get along – Project Happy Cats, I called it. More like *Scrappy* Cats, unfortunately."

"Oh dear," Amy said sympathetically. "That must be horrible."

Ella nodded. "I keep telling myself that Honey will probably be more sensible and calm when she grows up a bit, and they'll get on better … but I don't know if I can wait that long!"

Chapter 5

Molly's mum came in just then and smiled at them all. "Right! Shall we play some games?" she asked, putting six apples in the washing-up bowl, which was full of water. She put the bowl in the middle of the table. "Who fancies some apple-bobbing?"

"Me!" all six girls chorused, making Truffle jerk awake in surprise.

"I think I'd better take my nose off for this," Ella added with a chuckle, unhooking the elastic from around the back of her head. "Otherwise I won't get my mouth anywhere near an apple!"

Apple-bobbing was great fun … but hard work. It took a while for the girls to bite into an apple and bring it up out of the water in their teeth – and they all, Truffle included, managed to get splashed in the process.

Molly's mum had also hung up some marshmallows on strings, which they had to try to eat. It was more difficult than it looked, as the marshmallows kept swinging away from them, and Mia's beard ended up getting rather sticky. Truffle was fascinated by the dangling marshmallows and sat watching them, her blue eyes wide with interest.

Then they went into the living room to
play a Haunted House game where the girls
took it in turns to be blindfolded – and
have the others try to spook them! It was
quite nerve-racking, Ella thought, sitting
with a blindfold on, while the others made
creepy noises behind her, or brushed things
against her face to make her jump.

Just as they'd finished the game, there was
a great barking from outside, and the girls
heard the front door opening and lots of
loud voices. "Uh-oh," Molly said. "They're
back from football. Watch out, Truffle, the
boys are home, and so is Harvey."

The living-room door opened and in
lolloped a big, sandy-coloured dog with
friendly eyes and a wagging tail. "Hello,
Harvey," Lily said, giving him a pat.

Harvey made a rumbling woof in his
throat when he saw Truffle,
as if he were saying hello
to her, but Truffle was
already running from
the room. They
heard her cat flap
rattle moments later.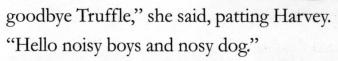
Molly sighed. "And it's
goodbye Truffle," she said, patting Harvey.
"Hello noisy boys and nosy dog."

"Tea's ready!" called Molly's mum just
then.

The Kitten Club girls went into the
kitchen to find a wonderfully spooky party
tea. There were witches' fingers (little
sausages), blood pizza (cheese and tomato),
and trolls' eyeballs (olives), as well as

squashed fly biscuits (chocolate chip cookies) and baby ghosts (meringues).

Molly's brothers were in the kitchen too, eyeing up the party food hungrily. "Hands off, Alfie," Molly's mum said to the tallest of the boys, whose hand was already hovering over the bowl of skin slices (crisps). "This is for the girls. You're having yours later. Boys, you're all filthy! Go and get those muddy things off, please."

"Awww, Muuuum," Molly's brothers moaned, traipsing out of the room.

"And Harvey, get your nose out of Truffle's food bowl!" Molly's mum added, shooing him away. "Honestly, boys and dogs, eh?" she said to the girls, rolling her eyes. "They're as greedy as each other!"

"We heard that!" came a shout from the hall.

The party tea was yummy and as she went home that night, Ella felt really happy to be a member of Kitten Club. They always did such cool stuff together, and the girls were the nicest friends you could ask for. Now she just had to persuade her *cats* to be friends too, and everything would be perfect!

SUNDAY

Happy Halloween! Have just had the BEST time trick-or-treating. Loads of us from our road went out together, all dressed up. Honey even came some of the way with me, just like a real witch's cat!

Was really sad to say goodbye to Grandma earlier - it's been brilliant having her to stay, and she's really helped me with the cats. And it's school again tomorrow. WORST LUCK! I am <u>so</u> going to miss Honey.

On Monday morning, Ella looked out for Mia in the school playground, but couldn't see her anywhere. Since Kitten Club had started, the girls had got to be really good friends and by break time, Ella was really missing her friend. She found Mia's big sister, Sunita, in the playground, who explained that Mia had a bad cold and was staying at home. Ella felt disappointed, especially as their teacher, Mrs Andrews, made her and Freya Walker, the meanest girl in class, partners for a new literacy project. Working with Freya was not at all fun. "Ella, you're *hopeless*," Freya kept saying loudly. "Your spelling is *awful*. Are you stupid or something?"

Ella gritted her teeth and tried not to get drawn into an argument. All the same, she was glad when it was home time, and Dad was there to walk her and Finn home. But when they arrived back at the house, she found that Misty and Honey were having a big argument of their own – a hissing, scratching argument on the kitchen floor!

"Whoa, major bust-up," Finn said, staring, but Ella was worried. This was a violent scrap even by Misty and Honey's standards. She hesitated, wanting to break them up, but not wanting another scratch for her trouble.

Just then Honey let out a yelp and cowered away, as if she'd been hurt. As Ella rushed over, Misty bolted out of the cat flap. Ella picked up Honey, then gave a cry of dismay. "Oh no! Look at her face!"

Chapter 6

The twins and their dad peered at poor
Honey, who had a bleeding scratch just
above her eye. "That looks nasty," Dad
said. "I think we should get the vet to check
her over."

Ella felt shaky just looking at the
scratch. If it had been a few millimetres
lower, it could have been Honey's *eye* that

was bleeding. "Honey, you have *got* to stop hassling Misty," she told her kitten as she put her gently into the cat-carrier. "I mean it. I know you only want to play, but you've got to leave her alone. Otherwise…" She bit her lip, not wanting to think about the "otherwise".

Dad, Ella and Finn took Honey along to the vet's. Luckily, it wasn't too busy and they could be seen quickly. The vet prescribed some antiseptic cream for Honey's scratch, and said it should heal up without any problems. "How can we stop the cats fighting?" Ella asked her. She told the vet they'd tried putting a bell on Honey's collar, keeping the cats apart where possible and giving Misty extra attention, but that they still weren't getting along.

"You've done all the right things so far," the vet said. "One other thing you could try is squirting water on them when they fight. All cats hate getting wet, and it'll break them up without you having to get scratched, at least. Once you've sprayed them a few times, you never know, they might get the idea that fighting is a bad thing."

"Cool!" Finn said, his eyes lighting up. "I've got a water pistol we can use."

Ella rolled her eyes at their dad. What was her brother *like*? Still, at least now he was going to help her break up the cat fights. It would make a change from him *starting* them half the time…

WEDNESDAY

Honey's eye is better again – phew – but things between her and Misty are as bad as ever. Honey just can't resist pouncing on Misty, and then Misty biffs her, and they're off again. Me and Finn are becoming good shots with the water pistol, though, and getting a soaking breaks up the fights really quickly. Mind you, Mum FREAKED when Finn squirted them in the living room and accidentally drenched the sofa. We've been told (v. strictly!) that we are only allowed to use the water pistol outside. Oops.

Other good news – Mia was back at school today. THANK GOODNESS! Was getting totally fed up with being stuck with mean Freya as a partner.

On Thursday after school, Mia came back to Ella's for tea. It was November now, but a lovely sunny afternoon so they put their coats on and took Honey into the garden, making the most of the sun before it started getting dark. "And we can keep her away from Misty out here," Ella said. "Come on, Honey-pie!"

Remembering what Lily and Ruby had said about their kittens loving playing with leaves, Ella scooped up a handful of leaves that had fallen from the birch tree, and let them drift from her hand so that they floated on to the grass in front of Honey.

Honey quivered with excitement. She crouched into a hunting position, wiggled her bottom and then gave a mighty spring on to the nearest leaf, rolling over on to her

side with it and kicking it with her back legs.

Ella and Mia both giggled. "I love the way they do that," Mia said. "They act as if they're lions stalking prey." She grabbed some more leaves and flung them into the air. "Look, Honey. More leaves to catch!"

Soon Honey was having a wonderful
time, pouncing on leaf after leaf as if she
were on a mission to fight every single one.
But all of a sudden, she froze. Her back
arched, her fur stood on end and her tail
fluffed up to twice its usual size.

"What's wrong?" Ella asked in surprise.
She turned to see what Honey was staring
at, and realized why her kitten was so
frightened. Nero, the big black tomcat from
two doors down, was on the wall that
divided Ella's garden from the one next
door. "Shoo," Ella said, flapping her hand
at him. "Go on, shoo!"

Nero didn't move. He stayed on the wall,
his yellow eyes narrowing as he stared at
Honey. "I'll get the water pistol," Ella
decided. "I'll be right back, Mia."

But Finn, seeing Nero through the kitchen window, had already grabbed the water pistol and was on his way out with it. "Cat SHOWER!" he yelled, spraying everything in sight. Within moments, Nero had vanished back next door, but the girls were soaked through, and poor little Honey was drenched too. With one terrified look at Finn, she scrambled up the nearest tree,

where she cowered on a branch.

"Finn!" Ella shouted furiously. "Now look what you've done!"

"Honey, come on, it's OK," Mia called, hurrying over to the tree. But Honey wouldn't come to her *or* Ella when they tried to coax her down. In fact, she edged away from them, going higher up in the branches, her eyes wide and fearful.

"Look at her, the poor thing, she's shivering with cold now," Ella said wretchedly. "Honestly, my brother is such an idiot sometimes! Come on, let's go and find Dad. He'll be able to reach her."

Dad managed to get Honey down by standing on a step-ladder. The girls took her inside and gently rubbed her with a towel until her fur was dry. But Honey didn't seem her usual bouncy self after her fright, and was clingy and timid for the rest of the day. Ella felt really cross with Finn. So much for him being helpful – by frightening Honey, he'd only gone and made things worse!

Chapter 7

When Ella woke up on Friday, she still felt annoyed by what her brother had done. Why did he have to be so loud and thoughtless all the time? She didn't speak to him at breakfast, or on the way to school.

That morning, Ella's class were busy practising their assembly for the following week. They had been learning about the

Romans, and their teacher, Mrs Andrews, had
written a short play about a Roman family
that they were to act out. Ella had been
chosen to play Flavia, one of the family's
slaves, and by a stroke of bad luck, Freya had
been picked to play Claudia, the mother, and
Ella's boss. Unfortunately, being Freya, she
took to the idea of bossing Ella around rather
too enthusiastically and couldn't resist
changing some of the lines as they rehearsed.

In the first scene, Ella, as the slave-girl,
had to assist Freya putting on her toga. Freya
stuck her nose in the air, rolling her eyes as
Ella tried to wind the white sheet over Freya's
school uniform. "Faster, Slave-girl, come on!"
she said. Then she pulled a face. "Honestly,
this slave is useless," she complained. "No
wonder nobody else wanted her."

"Hey!" Ella snapped. "Those aren't the right words!"

"Yes, stick to the script, please, Freya," Mrs Andrews said, looking up from her page. "Carry on."

After dressing her mistress, Ella-the-slave had to bring in a Roman breakfast. Mia, who was one of the narrators, said,

"Roman families would have bread, honey and fruit for breakfast. Very rich Romans might eat cheese and olives too. Their slaves would have a meal of bread and water."

"Hurry up, Slave-girl!" Freya ordered. "Get a move on!"

"It doesn't say that in the script, Freya," Mrs Andrews said sternly. "Do it properly."

Ella felt herself bristling as she set down the tray of plastic food. Why did Freya have to be so rude and horrible all the time?

Break time wasn't any better. Freya kept calling Ella "Slave-girl" all the time in the playground and giggling with her mates. "Slave-girl, come and do up my shoe for me!" she yelled. "Slave-girl, come and brush my hair, it's got tangled by the wind. *Now*, Slave-girl, or you'll get the sack!"

"Ignore her," muttered Mia. "She's just showing off."

Ella did her best to ignore Freya, but Freya seemed to be enjoying herself too much to stop. "Hey, Slave-girl! What have you got in your packed lunch today? As your mistress, I order you to give me any crisps or biscuits."

"No chance," Ella snapped, feeling as if she were about to lose her temper. "Come on, Mia, let's go and play somewhere else."

"Slave-girl, don't make me punish you!" Freya taunted. She and her friends were crowding in round Ella, mean smiles on their faces. "Remember what happens to bad slaves? They get beaten, or—"

She broke off suddenly, and Ella saw that Finn had appeared, his fists clenched. "Leave Ella alone," he shouted. "I mean it. If you speak to her like that again, you'll be sorry."

To Ella's surprise, Freya went pale and cast her eyes down. Finn was popular in their year and Freya clearly didn't want to get on the wrong side of him. Finn glanced over at Ella as Freya sloped away followed by her cronies. "Are you all right?" he said.

Ella blinked, feeling taken-aback. "Yeah. Thanks," she said after a moment.

"No worries," Finn said gruffly, then went back to playing football with his mates.

"Whoa," Mia said with a grin. "That shut Freya up, didn't it?"

Ella nodded, still a little stunned. It was rather an unusual feeling, being grateful to her brother for the first time in ages. Unusual – and kind of nice.

After school that day, Ella went up to her bedroom to practise her lines for the assembly. Even though Finn had put a stop to Freya's meanness, Ella really didn't want to mess up her part and look stupid in front of her. It was hard to concentrate, though, as her gaze kept drifting to the window, where she could see Honey pottering about in the garden. Ella smiled as Honey sharpened her little claws on the apple tree, explored the undergrowth and patted a tall clump of grass that was moving in the wind.

But her smile vanished as she saw Nero leap on to the dividing wall. Honey looked up and saw Nero, and immediately backed off nervously.

Ella banged on the window, hoping to scare Nero off, but he didn't bat an eyelid. He jumped down into the garden and padded towards Honey, his tail swishing menacingly. Feeling scared for her kitten, Ella jumped up from her chair and rushed downstairs. Honey looked so teeny in comparison to Nero. Ella had to rescue her!

Chapter 8

But when Ella opened the back door, she realized that someone else had already beaten her to the rescue mission. Ella watched as a fast-moving streak of grey fur shot across the garden ... and her mouth dropped open as she saw that it was *Misty*, hurtling to Honey's defence.

Ella stared, hardly able to believe her

eyes, as Misty charged right
at Nero, yowling furiously,
her tail big and bushy, and her
ears back. Then, even more
surprisingly, Nero turned tail at
the sight of Misty thundering
towards him … and scrambled
hurriedly back over the wall!

Misty slowed to a more dignified trot as she reached Honey's side. She gave Honey's fur a brisk, business-like lick as if to reassure the kitten that everything would be OK.

Ella beamed and hurried over to pet the brave cat. "Oh, Misty, well done," she said, stroking her and scratching her behind the ears just how she liked it. She still couldn't quite believe what had just happened. "Aren't you lovely, rushing to help Honey? What a good girl!"

Honey came closer to Ella so that she

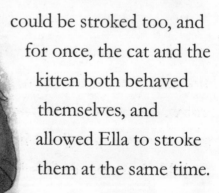

could be stroked too, and for once, the cat and the kitten both behaved themselves, and allowed Ella to stroke them at the same time.

Misty purred, and then so did Honey. Ella smiled, feeling very much like purring herself.

The next day was Saturday, and the six friends gathered at Mia's house for their Kitten Club meeting. Everyone loved hearing how Misty had leaped to Honey's defence to shoo away Nero. "It's a bit like you and Finn, isn't it?" Mia said with a smile. "You argue most of the time, but then when something serious happens, you stick up for each other."

"I suppose so," Ella said. She grinned. "And even though my brother is usually a massive pain in the bum, if a gigantic black cat was about to bully *him*, I guess I'd rush to his rescue, just like Misty did." She wrinkled her nose. "Well … probably.

I might be tempted to turn the water pistol on him for a bit first, of course…"

Everyone laughed. "That's really cool," Lily said. "I guess Misty must feel that Honey's part of the family now."

Ella nodded. "They're never going to be best friends," she said. "And I'm sure they'll still have the odd fight until Honey gets a bit older and calms down. But at least Misty feels Honey is worth sticking up for. And feeling as if they're both in Team Hughes is definitely a good thing!"

"Hooray for Misty," Ruby said, giggling as Mia's kitten Smokey clambered all the way up to her shoulder and began playing with the beads in her braids.

"And I'm glad Honey was OK. Our kittens have so many adventures, don't they?"

Amy grinned. "Non-stop," she said. "I wonder which kitten will have the next big adventure?"

"Not Smokey, I hope," Mia said, rolling her eyes. "He's already had enough to last him all of his nine lives!"

Just as Mia was saying that, Smokey, who was still playing with Ruby's hair, overbalanced suddenly and tumbled down into Ruby's lap, where he lay blinking up at her and looking rather surprised. "Oh, Smokey," Ruby laughed, stroking him. "You're not supposed to be having any more adventures! Don't you listen to *anything* Mia says?"

Smokey gave a meow as if to say a very

cheeky little "No!" and did a flying leap off Ruby's lap.

"More adventures coming right up," Ella said with a smile, as the lively kitten scampered across the room, his bright eyes seeming to search for something new to play with. "But that's why we love our kittens, right?"

"Right!" her friends all chorused as one.

Meow, went Smokey, as if agreeing, and everyone laughed.

Have you read...

Ginger's New Home

Smokey's Great Escape

Ziggy's Big Adventure